For Ramaben
—K. S.

For Eileen
—J. E.

Ω

Published by
Peachtree Publishing Company Inc.
1700 Chattahoochee Avenue
Atlanta, Georgia 30318-2112
www.peachtree-online.com

Text © 2020 by Kashmira Sheth
Illustrations © 2020 by Jeffrey Ebbeler

Edited by Kathy Landwehr
Design and composition by Nicola Simmonds Carmack

The illustrations were rendered in acrylics.

Printed in September 2019 by Tien Wah Press in Malaysia
10 9 8 7 6 5 4 3 2 1
First Edition
ISBN 978-1-68263-135-5

Library of Congress Cataloging-in-Publication Data

Names: Sheth, Kashmira, author. | Ebbeler, Jeffrey, illustrator.
Title: Feast of peas / written by Kashmira Sheth ; illustrated by Jeffrey Ebbeler.
Description: Atlanta, Georgia : Peachtree Publishing Company Inc., [2020] | Summary: In Dakor, India, Jiva looks forward to a feast of peas from his garden, but when they are stolen at harvest time, Jiva sets out to catch the thief.
Identifiers: LCCN 2018061617 | ISBN 9781682631355
Subjects: | CYAC: Gardening—Fiction. | Robbers and outlaws—Fiction. | Friendship—Fiction. | India— Fiction.
Classification: LCC PZ7.S5543 Fe 2020 | DDC [E]—dc23 LC record available at
https://lccn.loc.gov/2018061617

Feast of Peas

By **Kashmira Sheth**

Illustrated by **Jeffrey Ebbeler**

PEACHTREE

ATLANTA

Once upon a time, in the country of India, lived a man named Jiva.

Every day Jiva worked in his garden until the sun turned as red as a bride's sari.

Jiva planted carrots and beans, potatoes and tomatoes, eggplants and okra. But he was most excited about his peas. As Jiva planted them, he sang,

Plump peas, sweet peas,
Lined-up-in-the-shell peas.
Peas to munch, peas to crunch,
I want a feast of peas for lunch.

The peas were the
first ones to sprout.

Jiva hoed the rows,
watered the seedlings,
and waited.

Soon, the vines rambled over the soil.

Jiva weeded and watered the garden and waited some more.

In time, the plants were covered with delicate blossoms.

Birds flew overhead. Jiva scratched his head, wondering how to keep them away from his peas. Then Jiva snapped his fingers. He had an idea.

He built a scarecrow out of sugarcane stalks and dressed it with an old dhoti, a shirt, and a red turban.

Jiva waited some more.

The pea flowers turned into tiny peapods and the tiny peapods turned into big pods.

Soon it would be time for a feast of peas!

Ruvji came to visit. "Jiva, some of your peas look plump," he said, smacking his lips.

"I'll pick them tomorrow," Jiva said. "And then I'll have a feast of peas!"

He sang,

Plump peas, sweet peas,
lined-up-in-the-shell peas.
Peas to munch, peas to crunch,
I want a feast of peas for lunch.

"Peas are delicious," Ruvji said. "I would enjoy a feast of peas."

When Jiva got up the next morning, the sun was peeking over the horizon. He hurried to the garden to harvest the peas.

They had vanished!

Jiva examined the scarecrow. It still stood watch.

Just then Ruvji came by.

"Who ate my peas?" Jiva asked in a sad, soft voice.

"Maybe rabbits ate them," Ruvji said. "Look—there are some tiny peapods. Soon you'll have more peas."

Jiva scratched his head, wondering how to keep rabbits away. The scarecrow wouldn't help.

Then Jiva snapped his fingers. He had an idea.

Jiva put a fence around the garden.

A few days later, there were more peas in Jiva's garden.

Ruvji visited again. "Jiva, some of your peas look plump," he said, smacking his lips.

"Yes," Jiva said. "I'll pick them tomorrow. And then I'll have a feast of peas!" He sang,

Plump peas, sweet peas,
lined-up-in-the-shell peas.
Peas to munch, peas to crunch
I want a feast of peas for lunch.

"Peas are delicious," Ruvji said. "I would enjoy a feast of peas."

When Jiva got up the next morning, the sun was peeking over the horizon. He hurried to the garden to harvest the peas.

They had vanished!

Jiva examined his scarecrow. It still stood watch.

Jiva examined the fence. It was secure.

Just then Ruvji came by.

"Who ate my peas?" Jiva asked.

"Maybe a ghost ate the peas," Ruvji whispered. "Look—there are some tiny peapods. Soon you'll have more peas."

Jiva scratched his head, wondering how to keep the ghost away.

The scarecrow wouldn't help.

The fence wouldn't help.

Then Jiva snapped his fingers. He had an idea.

A few days later, Ruvji visited again. "Jiva, some of your peas look plump," he said, smacking his lips.

"I'll pick them tomorrow," Jiva said. He sang,

Plump peas, sweet peas,

Lined-up-in-the-shell peas.

Peas to munch, peas to crunch,

I want a feast of peas for lunch.

"Peas are delicious," Ruvji said. "I would enjoy a feast of peas."

The next morning just before the sun came out, a ghost appeared in the garden.

It stepped over Jiva's fence.

It bowed to Jiva's scarecrow and asked, "May I have some peas, please?"

Then the ghost answered his own question. "Of course, you may have as many peas as you please."

The ghost bowed again. "Why, thank you."

Quickly, he picked all the peas and dropped them in a pouch.

The ghost was about to leave when the scarecrow came alive. "May I take those peas you have picked?"

The ghost trembled.

The scarecrow answered his own question, mimicking the ghost's voice, "Of course, you may take all the peas."

The scarecrow extended his hands.

The ghost dropped his pouch.

As the scarecrow walked toward him, the ghost fled.

Down the street and up the alley,
the scarecrow chased the ghost.
They ran past the temple and through
the market. The ghost ran all the way
to the river. He dove into the water.

He looked back to see if the scarecrow was following him. Instead he saw a big crowd watching him from the shore. He had been tricked.

Ruvji took off his mask as he came out of the water. "Jiva, I'm sorry for stealing your peas."

"And trying to fool me, and scare me," Jiva said. "You must pay for what you have done."

Ruvji looked at the ground. "What's my punishment?" he asked.

Jiva scratched his head, wondering what to do. Then he snapped his fingers. "Ruvji, you can cook a feast for me," he said, smacking his lips.

Later that day, Ruvji shelled
and boiled the peas.

He steamed and simmered
the peas. He fried and
spiced the peas.

He made a feast of peas.

When Jiva sat down to eat, there were peas with rice and spice, peas wrapped in mashed potato pockets, and peas swimming in soup.

Jiva tasted the soup. "Delicious!" he said, taking another spoonful. Then he put it down and snapped his fingers. "You also love peas, Ruvji. Let's have a feast of peas together."

The two friends sang,

Plump peas, sweet peas,

Lined-up-in-the-shell peas.

Peas to munch, peas to crunch,

We have a feast of peas for lunch!